Metapatterning for Disconnection

Brandon W. Teigland

AOS Publishing 2023

Copyright © 2023

All rights reserved under International
and Pan-American copyright conventions.

ISBN: 978-1-990496-14-1

Cover Design: Jessica James

Visit AOS Publishing's website:
www.aospublishing.com

"You will never pray again, never adore again, never again rest in endless trust; you do not permit yourself to stop before any ultimate wisdom, ultimate goodness, ultimate power, while unharnessing your thoughts; you have no perpetual guardian and friend for your seven solitudes; you live without a view of mountains with snow on their peaks and fire in their hearts; there is no avenger for you any more nor any final improver; there is no longer any reason in what happens, no love in what will happen to you; no resting place is open any longer to your heart, where it only needs to find and no longer to seek; you resist any ultimate peace; you will the eternal recurrence of war and peace: man of renunciation, all this you wish to renounce? Who will give you the strength for that? Nobody yet has had this strength!"

– Nietzsche

On a desperate afternoon at the end of February, having returned from the underground laboratory in the Jinping Mountains of Sichuan Province, I arrived at my Beijing apartment, writes Théodore Ostrom, where I would have lived for a few months in simulation environments, surveying the most detailed maps of the distribution of dark matter in the universe – had I not received a call from an automated legal service informing me that my parents, my brother, and my sister had all died.

Your parents, brother, and sister were killed in an accident. A private family service will be conducted remotely by livestream on Sunday for any friends and relatives currently living outside the country or unable to attend due to restrictions on group gatherings.

I walked calmly to the window and looked down on the streets, where a blood rain was falling like red resentment upon the skyscrapers of the ultra-modern district of the city, upon the enormous imperial capital, as though an interplanetary dragon had been slain to feed the fields of the country and business was going on as usual, because in the end, what was really important was the market, the decisive factor was the demand for business. Because there was nothing to fear in business. Because the end was just business. And the end had come. Death had come. The loss was pure, instant, spherical.

With my hands in my pockets, I slowly circled the room. I had no clear sense of *what I had to do*. In my Beijing apartment, *what I had to do today* was unclear, and questionable. This unclear sense of *what I had to do* was the only constant. I couldn't just take the early morning flight home from China for the funeral because the lockdown and airline bans were in full effect. Something in me understood that I'd only know *what I wanted to do* when I discovered the importance, urgency, and immediacy of *what I had to do*.

So I envisioned myself at the airport in Beijing: I identified the counters and the gates, showed my vaccine passport for global travel, found the Chinese charter line, searched the runways for the baggage handlers and cargo crew, and tried to identify the pilot among the strangers waiting for the plane. My eyes followed him through a maze of paths in the construction site under the muddy drizzle that hovered over the city for the winter months. I located the seatbelt, studied the flight's literature. The infotainment system notified me that the flight took twenty hours. Then the plane took off across the wet runway, rose into the web of mist, and emerged into the sunlight above. To my left, the new sky was empty. To my right, the clouds hovering over the depths of outer space were streaked with cosmic radiation. Over a world with which I'd completely lost touch.

'How can I escape this fatal appointment?' I thought. I was troubled at the idea that the funeral couldn't take place at once and was sorry that my family weren't able to simply cybernetically extend their consciousness by uploading their minds to cloned bodies after their death. I sat down at my desk, turned on my computer, and read over the will. I'd been named executor. My inheritance had been left intact, which still had assets numerous enough to make the job of sorting it out terribly complicated. It would all have to be inventoried and appraised. Another headache. So much stood in my way. My deep ignorance of law, of investment, of real estate, ultimately of the dead family themselves, and I began to outline what I was in for: *Learn intimately the books and the business, go through probate, collect all debts, inventory the assets, get the estate appraised, decide what to liquidate and what to hold on to, pay off claims, square away taxes, distribute legacies . . .*

Life is not worth worrying about so much.

I opened a browser window, brought up various newspaper accounts, and clicked on the headlines "New Cases" and "Track World Curve" and "Timeline: How the Unknown Virus Spread." The number of estimated deaths was rising, with many more confirmed cases. Not surprised, I refreshed the home page and watched the number of new cases change.

I couldn't imagine entering another human city again, another infected human city. It was the worst time to be in any city. I didn't want to leave my Beijing apartment, afraid that all this, so impermanent, so fake, would disappear. I saw no faces outside my window, as there were none, just the long streets with no business, no pedestrians, no vehicles. It was so empty that it seemed as if I were looking at a diorama.

Another wave of variants will come, I thought, and with it another lockdown. Unable to endure the isolation any longer, people will leave their homes to huddle together, in shared isolation. In masses united by incomprehension of this futuristic flu that deprived them of all meaning. For fear of the worst death, everyone must avoid these polluted people. These polluted people will be treated in much the same fashion as sacred persons, and in return they must observe stricter and stricter restrictions – restrictions that don't apply to other people.

I'd read the accounts of collapse on my laptop, of the fundamental paranoia of nations and the dirge for a world brought into confusion and error. Because all the paper money was thrown out or lost its value. Devalued, the entire world's currency, in the banks, the vaults, was exchanged for zeros. Now it's not only virtual funds circulating in the electronic space but also a social credit system that gives every one of its citizens a personal score on how they behave.

I'd accessed an array of libraries, journals, and news services. Opposing this mendacious world with the resources of irony without illusion, demonstrators formed groups and attacked cars, turning them over and setting them on fire. Military police stood guard with riot guns and tear gas, shooting into the mob until the situation deteriorated.

The Beijing news media gestalt called the Chinese protests "riots" when really they should have been called "protests," I thought, whereas the dangerous demonstrations in the United States were called "protests" but should have been called "riots."

The protests, so the news said, remained in the throats of most people. Here and there were the flames from Molotov cocktails, shots, violence. A massive chorus singing. Banners fluttering in the breeze. Voices that seemed to come up through the bathtub drain or the toilet hole. Groups shouting threateningly through loudspeakers, groups with arms linked, streaming endlessly by. They gave in to their hatred. The worst of illusions. And they rushed off toward a thousand other unruly acts that have made all the more hateful a humanity already degraded by an excess of hatred.

I didn't actually see the demonstrations, but when I heard about them on the internet, I felt that things wouldn't end here, and that larger-scale riots had to be in store for the future. I cannot think of a future...

By every indication they were attacking their own country. Armed insurrection. Things would cease only with the end of human freedom, or with a communist government that, after stripping away everything inessential to human freedom, would unite progress with a frozen human life. A classless society is the direction history has taken. We have the convulsions of the communist horizon always before us. No one can escape from one system without being immediately obliged to adopt another system that is just as closed, or more so. If the East is post-communist and the West is post-capitalist then what is the world?

The evidence of war dominated the certitude of peace. War will soon be unavoidable. As a result of the World Wars, first Russia and then a whole series of countries in the European East and Asia dropped out of the system of capitalism. The world without war rotted, and there was every reason for me to assume, as I did, that a Third World War would bring about the total collapse of world capitalism.

My brother believed that no matter how things arrived in the present, the possible futures were absolutely fixed with memory. I, on the other hand, forget everything, purposely forget, remaining without memory, assuming that no future could ever depend on random information from the past but only on relevant information about the current time. Because like a nucleus, the present moment in us does not age with the passage of time, and no matter how long the present has existed, or how different the new now is for each of us, its disintegration doesn't change it. Human lives break down, I thought, and this breakdown only increases from the moment we begin our existence. For me decay and decline hold no fear. I know that I will die and that I will rot.

It's human to be monstrously hopeless, I thought. The world feels secure when reality feels monstrous. No matter what is done to destroy violence, violence manifests in myriad forms: physical violence, sexual violence, the violence of emotions, psychological violence, spiritual violence, the violence of culture, verbal violence, the violence of finance or the economy, the violence of neglect, and self-directed violence, of love, of hate, of indifference. And the only source of it all is life: violence exercised on inertia.

We are fated to extirpate ourselves, root and branch, I thought. Nothing is so predictable as this violent response to the decay of a society grown old, this anarchy of responsibility. I myself am without doubt a part of it. What distinguishes me is my uncommon sense of observation. I might not have any resentment beyond all this violence, but a mute demand does remain within me. This demand remains fixed to the world, while I drift farther and farther away from this planet.

Then I read the reports of my family's accident. The names appeared to me as no more than hollow words. *The car braked suddenly at the Cabot Trail turnoff and plowed through the guardrail and into the Cabot Strait. Everyone inside the car drowned. The owners of the neighbouring houses were keeping away from their vacation villas along the highway, I read, frightened by rumours that outsiders were no longer wanted, which was why the accident wasn't reported sooner.*

Behind the reports I couldn't find reasons for these individuals to go out of existence. I couldn't find reasons for the improbable accident that made these individuals cease to exist. Death is never natural but requires a magical explanation.

My brother was at the wheel, I thought, after I finished reading all the coverage I could find on the accident. They had let him drive knowing full well that he was prone to episodes. My mother must have been arguing with him while he was driving. She was notorious for arguing him into paralysis, and according to all the reports, she'd been right beside him, in the passenger seat.

I could no longer turn back my state of exhaustion with any measure of nourishing liquids or electrolyte drinks, protein or carbohydrate supplements, vitamins or minerals. My body stung and throbbed with minuscule torments that weighed down on me. I felt weary and exhausted, and there was nothing to do but suffer. After taking a bath and lighting a cigarette, I felt slightly better. I can still smoke a cigarette, I thought. But it could be no more than a joyless diversion. I coughed a couple of times. There was a sour and nauseating taste in my mouth and after a while, in the middle of my second smoke, it really began to disgust me. When I started coughing again, I stopped and scowled.

Several seconds passed before the scene beyond the window registered through my bored tension and unhappiness. From the bathroom window, I saw the mephitic breath of the entire business district of Beijing in a reddish-brown light that cast no shadows. The dirty part of the sky expanded and rose, pushing away the blue bloom of the sky. The whole area was crowded with media-generated representations, holographic advertising inducing consumers to imagine that synthetic drugs would bring them good health, that cellular phones would break down the walls of isolation, and that vacations would restore the land and the ocean to them. They wanted consumers to console themselves with the idea that this paltry forgery, this fraudulent, counterfeit luxury surrounding them was really theirs to wallow in, that it existed, that it was real, atmospherically. In whatever direction I looked, the city appeared more and more deserted, the surroundings more desolate, and I was overcome by an unbearable sense of loneliness.

Like a plague god above the sun there was a huge QR code suspended in midair, to which I paid particular attention and scanned, considering the situation further. The spread of the novel virus and its variants, a global speciation event, which science decorously supplied with Greek names, had taken a turn for the worse – the initial steep, jagged upward curve, then the few steps back down, and then the steady high plateau that fell above its previous standard level. It was an infection that, in its stubbornness and seriousness, was out of proportion to any medical finding, remaining beyond evaluation, or so the medical experts said.

Twice a month, I had to report an antigen test. Every three months, I administered yet another shot to boost my immunity, inserting the needle and squeezing the syringe. The injections were hard on the system, evidenced by an immediate, though momentary, rise in temperature. It all happened as per regulation, with no deviations from the norm. The vaccine was under the skin, in the arm.

Life is a body ripe for viruses. To be flesh and blood is problematic, I thought. To be stuck in your skin, to be merely entrails in a skin and then, having given your skin up to medicine, to no longer have that skin to yourself, to be forever hidden away behind a body, and the functional extremities of the heart, neurons, and immune system in which it begins and ends, like a knot that cannot be undone, binding us to a plot larger than ourselves – a plot where we are bound to our own body as others are bound to their bodies.

I had a sudden vision of the unceasing torments inflicted on humanity by the virus. From generation to generation, every living creature will hand down the inexhaustible heritage of this viral infectivity. This everlasting disease will ravage the descendants of humanity and will even be in the bones of our fossils, dug up by them in the future. It will continue to travel down the ages and will still be ravaging our nonhuman successors in the form of pains, in the disguise of headaches or bronchitis.

In one remote corner of the vast sea of disinformation on the Internet, there were groups who thought that people like me, an alleged speciation sympathizer by my association with the foreigner caste of the intelligentsia here in China, had no defence against the genetically altered virus. Supposedly I was its target.

Once infected, it would create fatal toxins in my blood. Of course it was highly infectious, spreading quicker and quicker across the globe, and would probably strike me in the end. Those who had produced this frightening weapon of genetic assassination didn't even need to know where I was. All they needed to do was spread the virus in my general vicinity. Because, while it caused little to no illness in ordinary people, a mild flu at most or respiratory infection, it had the ability to recognize me, in a sense, as a particular individual, identifying me by my genetic characteristics.

My dread of this disease will bring on the disease itself if I keep this up, I thought, so I put on something to listen to: *Lamento di Glossolalia.* The digital cover art for this lamento popped up, revealing a complex, almost hallucinatory painting of an eighteenth-century style dance party in a European palace hall. All the dancers had their eyes closed. Under a great unlit chandelier, each couple on the floor of the grand ballroom appeared to be dancing to whatever was in their heads, a choreography in which each couple meshed easily, predestined, waiting for the collisions to begin, though none ever came.

I followed the music anonymously. And after a few minutes, I already detested it. My hands simply lay open in the tepid bath water, grasping nothing, stirred, occasionally, by the rhythms of the song. The insipid, symmetrically fashioned melody echoed euphoniously through the growing darkness, and periodically my lips whistled along in a whisper.

Death's invitation to look back on the life of my family loomed large. So, to the accompaniment of endless waves of music, both mournful and tender, I gave it a try, just to see if it would do me any good. The memories were limited and waning. I tried to think of them as my family, no longer seeing anything in them but this word. The word *family* denotes blood ties. But if I say that they, who are now analogous to inert things, are my family, this is in order to be assured that they are like me. But we are different in our distance from death. In all their bloodless and rigid substantiality, their stored, coded personalities have met an early death.

After the death of the people who are closest to us, everything becomes like a corpse, I thought. The definitive impotence and absence of death is everywhere. We die into the world. We feel and smell the putrid corpse it is turning into. A road is not a road but the corpse of a road. A home is not a home but the corpse of a home. A family is a corpse. A country and its people, too, are corpses. For weeks, all we see are corpses. Our world is a pregnant corpse. So that even we ourselves become corpses.

I ordered a delivery drone to bring me a bottle of Chinese vodka. In a few minutes, a small, flying delivery drone pulled up outside the transparent wall and delivered the alcohol through the portal that opened. I drank shots in my bathrobe until I began to feel light-headed. I then lay on the sofa with the music still on, staring at the air multiplier, a large ceiling fan mounted above me blowing air from a ring with no external blades. Bladeless. Reminiscing drunkenly about my past.

I thought vaguely that I needed to wash my hands again, and as I did so, I wondered when it was that I'd first fallen into the habit of washing my hands after each brush with humanity, to avoid being contaminated. When it came to containing the disease, progress was slow and torturous. Terror only grew. And a palpable fear reigned. The disease knew where it was going, I sensed. Digital machines computed in advance the complex web of its spread, but not fast enough, and I knew only that it might reach me at any moment, whatever I did.

Rather than taking to my bed and resorting to a heavier dose of synthetic drugs than usual, not knowing whether I'd wake up again, I thought it would be better to satisfy myself with a more ordinary escape and go online shopping instead. The table was thick with vials, bottles of liquor. I put the plastic vials of red pills back on the table, pondered the indecipherable hieroglyphics of their names for a moment or two. Instead, I dissolved them in the Chinese vodka for later.

Online, I picked out the proper garment for the virtual funeral, something cuffless and collarless. Along with the grey Zhongshan suit, I purchased a small pair of black Japanese binoculars and a Chinese zun. Most vendors sold the same stuff and all overcharged for disinfection. I browsed bogus wholesale Chinese schlock bought from imitation manufacturers. Their new merchandise – knockoff running shoes, jeans, piles of commodities – neatly displayed the logos of international companies and seemed to represent the whole fake market.

By the time my orders had been delivered by another drone, it was growing dark but not yet time to turn on the lights. A gentle glimmering darkness lay over the room. Beneath me, I sensed the night in the heated stone floor, in the core of an earth without a fixed equator. Nothing but total solitude. I could hear only my watch softly ticking, in a silence unbroken even by the cry of a bird, for at that height no bird was to be found.

I put on the tunic suit I purchased and poured the rest of the vodka into the zun. Then, on the sofa, I moved as close as possible to the edge of the window. The vista stretched to a point beyond a wall of dirty sky. Off in the obscurity, in the circle of my binoculars, were the lights of Zhongnanhai.

There are tall buildings here, and although their foundations have been dug by the Chinese, these luciferous towers are really fortified observation towers, I thought. So much so that the top floors of not only my building but the upper storeys of all buildings in the area had been completely expropriated by the national security authorities of either the Americans or the Europeans or the Japanese or the Chinese, since Zhongnanhai, which serves as the central headquarters, could not only be seen but closely monitored from that height. The world gets used up from being seen too much, I thought, and for hours I simply looked out my Beijing apartment window at Zhongnanhai.

There is a false quality to our existence as humans. It's as if we know we're constantly being watched and have begun, like living actors, to act out our small parts – parts that come to resemble a theatrical performance, so that at the end of our lives we are neither human nor actor but a mere automaton dressed in the same human costume. That is how humans are.

When I found my face reflected in the window, I was surprised to see I was almost a couple of weeks into raising a beard. What had become of me in this city of Beijing, where I had neither relatives nor friends? Theoretically, a person with a supply of stored food, drugs, supplements, and antibiotics could live out the famine and disease. If I escape death in the sense that I do not die fleeing, I thought, then I will die from not dying.

Funny situation.

Perhaps I will soon walk on all fours, tip down onto my front limbs, and begin to grunt. I could go back to animal behaviour and take that burning step backward, a lost animal, lost in an alien world. Yet another creature of the earth dying from the world. I am a human, and humans live and die like animals do.

I gradually sharpened the focus on my binoculars, to cut through the machine air, and stared into the red darkness of the rain at Zhongnanhai. A furious rain that threw itself like an avalanche on Beijing and in which viruses and infections proliferated.

Then I attempted to recall the earliest scenes of my life. It all came back to me in a stream of sensations that rippled on the surface of my body and rattled down my spine. Everything flowed into everything else. Reflections flowed into reflections, into years of water, into hours of wind. It rained thought and death, unending and without purpose. It rained, and without realizing it, I wanted to dissolve into tears, into intimacy, and into ugly laughter.

I'd never had any awareness of my proper place with my family, a family that could withdraw far from city life whenever they wanted. I'd always felt a nameless irritation for them all. Whenever I thought about my family, I began to lose my identity. My earliest days were spent brooding in the shade of the porch of their villa, in the Cape Breton Highlands, in the worst little town of all the seacoast towns on the eastern edge of Canada. From spring to fall, I sat in the shadow of the porch. I must be my support and go on living alone, I'd thought then, sitting on that terrace, because we are always alone when we are living in someone else's life. Later, I left to study in China and never saw my family again.

I couldn't quite get into my head that the day I left to study in China was the day I saw my family for the last time. I had turned my back on them all, cruelly and sullenly. I should have despised myself, for I'd disowned myself by going away. I should have felt a sense of having done something irreparable to my family.

The Jinping Mountains acted as my shield against the world. After finishing graduate school, I used a face-scanning algorithm on a recruitment system that used my computer's camera to analyze my facial movements, word choice, and speaking voice before ranking me against other applicants based on an automatically generated employability score, and I immediately got a job with China Jinping Underground Laboratory. The inertia mines in the mountains of Sichuan became like a second home to me. A place where I could safely bury myself in research, nearly a mile underground, in my analytical basement, hunting the ghosts of hypothetical particles.

Even now, I can imagine myself going into these caves. I can feel the narrow passage, the closely packed pipes running everywhere, growing like the stalks of a hollow vine along the walls. I can even put my hand on the giant detector and try to understand the signals I'm seeing – the nuclear moments that glow like abstract clocks against the dark background of those cavernous halls, thousands of feet beneath the earth, where absolute cosmic silence reigns. In the interminable silence of that cosmic bastille there is a silence as fearful as the eternal silence of unknown space. Gazing at this dazzling dark force, I experience the miraculous fulguration of an unavowable moment whose reality the light prevented me from seeing. And I could not free myself of the thought that not only the particles but the place itself had disappeared forever. After all, I was the one who had witnessed it and now, only I would know what it looked like. Only I would remember.

Our bodies know we should not ever see it.

My theory is that, because we are hardwired with a hominid brain, every glimpse of anything not descended from that original hominization will fail to see dark matter. Because here among forms that lacked the conviction to moan, there was a universal negation that could not be hidden – this immense negation that situated us in the universe in the way cancer inscribes itself in a body. The negation leaves nothing existing above it, below it, beside it, inside it. There was just this negation, and that was all. An ephemeral concentration of something immaterial, of energy, of something not yet matter but related to matter, of something that one could no longer think of as matter but rather as both the medium and boundary between the material and the immaterial. It was the inexhaustible matter of our own bodies, matter that would return to matter, that knew the universe and knew itself as extraterrestrial.

I returned to my tiny Japanese binoculars once more. They were for nature observation. But I can't see myself using them to observe nature, I thought, and went on thinking about how limited Beijing's ecosystem was. I've never even seen a bird in Beijing. I tried to discern the Japanese aesthetic principles of wabi, sabi, and yūgen, but either my mind was too loud or my eye not cultivated enough for such subtle signs of nature. Nature doesn't appear. It doesn't appear in the overarching patterns of patterns, not in spheres, sheets, tubes, borders-pores, layers, binaries, centres, calendars-time, arrows, breaks, or cycles, and it does not appear when you consider other metapatterns such as gradients, clusters, voids-space, rigidity, emergence, webs-networks, or triggers. The vague notion of nature as a way of exploring the fundamental connectedness of the phenomenal world is useless. All nature is useless to me except as a science. Nature ends with the word *science* in the same way that language ends with the word *God*.

Then I thought about the woods of my childhood. No one besides my sister and me had played in them. We climbed trees, entwined our legs around branches, and swung up and down, crushing the green cytoplasmic substance of plants or scattering the superimposed stages of leaves toward the ground as we jumped, like a pair of birds or winged insects invading the sky. The world was there, with its forests and animals in all their innocence, and only this world was real. There the world fell in two. As children, unaware of our parents' hopes, we still played games of hide-and-seek with eternity. Time hadn't yet started. Infinity revealed itself to us for the first time. Because in the movement of our living animal matter, basically the same as the plants', was unending time. We were nothing but growth, nothing but a wild exuberance.

This exuberant beauty was in the damp spring stars. In the many years of cold rain rippling across the screen of cypresses. In the brambles and the rose bushes. In the rabbit nibbling its way through the garden and the doves murmuring in the vines and shade. In the alpine valleys. In the bays and among the highlands. In the clouds and the eagles, the wind, and the rising sun. In the roots of the chestnut tree, in the ferns and the ghost pipe, in the spores of lion's mane, in the sterile conk of chaga. In the rocky cliffs that rose sovereign. In the rocks over which mountain goats leaped. In the trenches of seaweed. In the crushed stones and shells from the beach. In the brush-covered resting places of deer. In the hulks and ruins of empty estates, abandoned and alone with lichen on the stucco. In the towns glistening in the heat and in the cheerful, serene sound of cathedral bells. In automobiles and pedestrians. In the children and the old people.

When we are no longer children, we become disposed to think about how the world must be in terms of facts. But as adults we can say nothing about the world, except that it's objectively mysterious. Because a child feels more than an adult knows, and because a child knows more than it feels. Since childhood, I've made nothing but corrections to my knowledge of the world, and yet the world remains unaffected by all these corrections. As a matter of fact, I don't know what the world is and I would not be able to produce another one by any means. To the extent that we forget that we are ourselves the world, we deny it. But it is ourselves that we deny. Without being anywhere, it may flare up in anything, at any place. For all things draw us – even those who find it difficult to accept it – toward it more rapidly, more clearly, more beautifully.

The Zhongnanhai produced nothing at all. The building was a parasitic structure. Outside the Zhongnanhai complex, which I could see only partially from my floor, military police stood guard while party members absentmindedly smoked cigarettes and cigars or strolled through the former Imperial Garden in the Imperial City, adjacent to the Forbidden City, like so many idle lords or substitute kings or fake monarchs. I tried to imagine a subjective existence in the heads of these humans, the privacy of a conscious existence, but could not. At the same time, a revolution was occurring within them.

No, I had not yet settled into China, not in terms of my intimacy with life here. As a stranger to post-communism, I still needed to reveal to myself what was hidden behind such militant convictions: a class-based divide between masses who work for algorithms, a privileged professional class who have the skills and capabilities to design and train algorithmic systems, and a small, ultrawealthy aristocracy who own the algorithmic platforms that run the world.

The truth is that, not understanding the society I took part in, I neither welcomed nor rejected this unquestioning doctrinal submission that placed the fate of the world at issue. I merely treated it like a dead idea stretched out on a dissecting table. The cause was given: it was for their purpose that I was here. I was summoned into their setting, to sink into it, into the depths of Chinese science. To forget the rest and devote myself to it. I led myself to the designs of a foreign will and allowed myself to be appropriated. For me, there was nothing beyond this cabal of scientists in China. They could dispossess me of my work, take it or buy it, and so direct my very behaviour.

We cannot make just anywhere our home. Home is always somewhere else when we are nowhere. Despite all our adventures, we remain on our way home. From time to time I still wished to go back. But could I take on the responsibility of sending myself home once all the restrictions were lifted and return to a relation with a reality so distant from my own? I knew that it couldn't last forever. I knew that the void would soon open beneath my feet if I assumed so. I knew that, in that moment, I would experience not only my own dissolution but the dissolution of everything. Still, I would have liked there to have existed a place, a stable place, unmoved and unmoving, untouched and untouchable, unchanged and unchanging. A place that might be a point of *ursprung*. My own origin. My true home.

In general I was disgusted by the monotony of my life and had plans to depart. I was impatient to leave but had put it off time and again since coming to China, partly out of laziness and partly out of dislike of the trouble involved. We live out our lives as though we are already finished with them, I thought, though the time spent living our lives is always unfinished time. We may be finished with time but time is not finished with us. We have no idea where time is going. Time goes where it wants. And if time is dark, then we cannot provide a theory of temporality but instead grope blindly through the relativity of space.

Why have I not stopped or even eliminated time? A pathetic wish to remove time as a fundamental aspect of reality. A strange temporal itch. Probably a result of the solitary and routine nature of my work. There are hardly any people in my solitary life. Theories of physics don't include people, yet I still accept that people exist. Why? Because I can assume that people emerge from an underlying physics of particles whizzing around the universe, that they exist at a higher level than the level described by physics. But while people might be made of fundamental particles, I have no idea how time might be made out of something fundamental. Time might not exist at any level.

Is there any chance at all for the creation of a new metaphysics?

There is no way out of this mess. Our entire lives are built around time. We plan for the future in light of what we know about the past, and we believe ourselves to be people who can do things, in part, because we can plan to act in a way that will bring about changes in the future. But what's the point of acting to bring about a change in the future when, in a very real sense, there is no future to act for? When there is no past and so, apparently, no such action there either? Perhaps time doesn't exist and causation, the sense that one thing can bring about another, is the basic feature of our universe. Then I would have no reason to get out of bed.

I have two enemies: time and space. I have escaped the first, but the one I retain troubles me more than the one I've lost. I promised myself that in *Disconnection*, the book I was planning, I would find a way of drawing attention to these contingencies. I'd write, *If Newton's and Einstein's theories of gravity are wrong, then there are no laws of physics, no theories of physics, no models or transitions between theories of physics to guide us. Because*, I'd note, *there is no replacement for science but to feel that nothing is immutable.* It's my duty, I thought, to write about this in my *Disconnection*. And my *Disconnection* will prove the best opportunity to do this.

Once these descriptions are finished, the evidence of my experiments will be presented in the form of measurements. If my measurements are correct, we will have to look at the possibility of new physics, a new physical theory to explain the universe, propelling physics into a new era. Suppose such a theory turns out to be correct. These measurements would then construct a map that could show how patterns of dark matter sprawl across the universe. The black areas of this map would be vast areas of nothingness called voids, holes in the distribution of galaxies, regions in which matter is escaping and where the laws of physics might be different. The bright areas, where dark matter is supposed to be concentrated, called halos because of their gravity-distorted light, would then be galaxies like our own. Our reality, existing right in the centre of these halos.

Ninety-five percent of mass is not anything that we know. A mass mirage. A crowning illusion. Some new thing, some exotic thing, which at the moment is still nothing but a swirl of scattered exotic particles. So to give some kind of form and substance to a material composed of particles that cannot be seen directly, particles that don't absorb, reflect, or emit light, would mean we might be able to finally see it.

We know how much dark matter there is because it's got this immense influence due to gravity. But it exists in isolation and is, in this sense, exotic, without a world. Denying this is denying our universe. If it weren't there, we wouldn't have that extra gravity, which is created by dark-matter particles and is necessary to form the structure of the universe today. So there's tons and tons of evidence. However, a question without an answer, as they say, is a king without a throne.

Gravity is only one of the four fundamental forces of nature available for dark matter to interact with. Because we know it doesn't interact electromagnetically, we call it dark. It also doesn't interact through the strong nuclear force that holds atomic nuclei together because atoms wouldn't be stable and then we'd be dead. Basically we're left with having to find dark matter directly and, for us to do so, these particles need to occasionally interact with normal matter through the weak nuclear force, allowing them to be spotted by extremely sensitive detectors as they undergo radioactive decay.

An immense project, I went on thinking. Technically realizable. But an effort whose sole result, whose sole profit, will be the yearly maintenance budget alone. And like the construction of Versailles or Donzère-Mondragon Dam finally made a revolution inevitable, exemplifying a whole pattern of human relationships based on betrayal and hate, the rampant acceleration of technical progress will either represent the possibility of improved relationships or make the militarized organization of revolutionary tension inevitable.

The terrain of science can be disinterested. Disinterestedness allows us to separate truth from ideology, faith, and even science. But the horseshoe-shape of our post-ideologically way of thinking about truth only ever bends us back toward the truth of yet another post-truth ideology. The truth cannot be spoken. We cannot say what is true. Neither can we say what is not true. Truth is something which you cannot speak.

You cannot get to the end of things.

The situation doesn't change when a manifest form of science is abolished and diminished forms, bogus forms, succeed it. To do science is to disregard the present with a view to future results. Science begins by running up against this tide of scientists devoted to the relativity of a forever-unfinished science. Once the results are obtained, the science isn't done. Science is never done. Because the pupil of science is forever dilating. It's not a sudden illumination or a prize. Nothing appears to us in full except as a result at the end of a calculation. Science can't in any way be confused with the last moment or the end of the operation. It's the entire operation. To know is to strive. It's always an operation, indefinitely resumed, indefinitely repeated.

But no one can solve a problem like this in a post-communist regime. The government can't do anything. Nor can the scientists. They don't even think about it. They do not sense that there is a problem. Nothing even seems problematic to them. They only sense that there is progress.

There is no reconfiguring the entanglement I am in.

I gradually ceased to tax myself with these problems of science because, increasingly, I have become obsessed with them. It's frightening to be alone, to know nothing and have no proof, to feel the questions fall into the silence and the void without an answer. What shows itself? What?! What is it? What is it that it is?! This what, which has already wholly enveloped me, has eyes only for me. It is always awake. It is always looking at me. Everything in it looks at me.

Our ears didn't evolve to hear the human voice, I read on the packaging that described the binoculars, but birdsong. Birdsong is the primary indicator of habitats prosperous to humans. I considered this. Architecture should make buildings sing. And yet, I'd never heard or even seen a bird in all of Beijing, only increasingly citified millennials, a millennial abyss, where everything was adapted to the goal of production, full of smoke, full of waste and sadness. This city which spoke to itself in a monologue of twenty million voices.

I did not experience the melody of birdsong. And because no twittering of birds could be heard, nothing created within me the feeling that I would ever again return to nature.

I was removed from reality.

The time was about three or four in the morning or maybe not even that. The Chinese vodka I was drinking was having no effect on me. Or maybe I was drunker than I realized. The zun was thick. I tried to feel as drunk as possible. But this didn't work. I grew vaporized in a sort of intoxication, in a vague etherization.

My family never forgave me for becoming a scientist. They went on to claim that I was a member of the scientific caste. But I've been useful, I thought, and recalled the use I made of the money I earned in China. I extended my hand to them, or rather my science extended a hand to them. Not knowing whether to believe in my science, my family turned down the corners of their mouths, as if to say they didn't care to say another word. Because my family was always wary of believing in science, as if this would have deprived them of a capability to lead a genuine spiritual life. They didn't believe in science, calling it monistic, for it was a faith, they said, like any other.

If it was within the course of doing *what I wanted to do* that the material structures of my life determined a sequence of events, then it's true that I found myself in my own way. I'd moved to China with the conviction that my eyes saw what they were made to see, in the same way that my family had found the ignorant messiah they were made to worship.

One must proceed from clarity and not belief, and I've never been sufficiently clear in my beliefs. I am, at best, only an indifferent scientist who lives and moves without motive power. I believe in nothing more than the emergent self-organization of smaller things, coming and going in a quantum foam, popping in and out of a generative void.

My father devastated his children by bringing out a sense of metaphysical shame in us, a crushing, stifling, maddening shame for existing that could only become our accursed share of unique illnesses. I still feel the pain of respect, something like the pain of fear, when I think of him. In our father's proximity we felt ashamed to be thirsty or hungry. How deeply each of us loathed our hunger and the food our body craved. In my father's presence we felt ashamed of anything that might bring us the least pleasure. Only suffering held meaning for us. This presence is still in society with me – the presence of my father, who, by his words, permitted me to be.

Eating isn't much more than an opportunity to look down on those who don't eat. And it was this source of a sense of superiority that I couldn't and wouldn't throw off when considering my father's character and person. He almost always came late for meals, and until he arrived I would sit there with angry eyes. Even the memory of this dreadful part of my childhood still makes me lower my head over my plate when I'm eating, still makes my eyes travel around the rim of my plate. But I no longer really have a right to be angry.

My sister had anorexia for over a decade, even approached death on several occasions. In despair, she'd opened her arteries. She'd recovered only because she'd been convinced of my brother's love for her and so shared his strength, his confidence, his well-being and naivete. By loving my sister as she suffered, I thought, my brother became her true healer.

I dislike being pitied. In fact, I hate being pitied, while my sister accepted pity as a kind of medicine, even from me, in its lowest form. I'm no healer. I view sick people the wrong way. When I looked down upon her from the head of the hospital bed, the expressive patterns in her eyes and the smiling mouth my brother looked for didn't exist for me, and if I kept looking down on her I'd end up seeing a material mass with a teeth-filled flash on top and two wet spheres rolling in their sockets below.

The wind outside blew, striking the sharp corners of the building, moaning like a great pipe organ. I concentrated fixedly on Zhongnanhai without blinking. The iron fist is in its velvet glove, I thought. When the guards who'd stepped away finally returned, I saw someone who resembled no one, a faceless stranger, the very opposite of a being. One of them seemed not to have eyes. But the strain made my hallucinated eyeballs feel hot to the point of pain and so I stopped. I didn't wish to spy on them any further. But I couldn't sleep at all. I was sick of the loft and my limbs felt cold and disconnected.

I never sleep at night.

When I can't sleep, I need someone to talk to. (0) was the only person to understand this about me, themselves a seeker of the night that awaited no day. Into the depths of those nights totally foreign to human days we'd talk and talk, and when the sun came up, feeling as we did the sweet inactivity of those who cannot sleep, we sometimes felt like committing suicide. We lived on tea and grief and then took pills. But every time we woke up.

Nothing had happened. And we'd be disappointed we hadn't died. "There's so much to talk about if you know that it's going to be your last conversation," (0) would say. "And if the world is going to end tonight and you're still alive the next day, you just talk it all over again the next night."

On a holographic display light, I'd created an infinite loop of holographic photos and video messages of our relationship that were brought to three-dimensional life. These finely detailed spectral reflections of the real world reproduced both real and synthetic 3D information more realistically than any conventional 2D display. These were physically present holograms. Holograms I could touch. A touch that resembled vision.

I'd captured these holograms on my phone's holographic camera then created and configured playlists on the display light. I watched a ten-second holographic birthday message from (0) describing a dance-theatre piece of them in which the concept of a birthday wish is enacted by a dancer lighting cupcake candles in succession, then drawing the small flame nestled in each cupcake to the dancer's chest and extinguishing it.

I also kept an album of about twenty nude photographs that I'd taken of (0) over the years on this personal holographic display. I looked intently at these playful, provocative nudes, however silly. I didn't feel the least ashamed for having kept them instead of destroying them. I liked to fondle these images, gloomy or iridescent by turn, that my restless and avid imagination only revealed to me poorly. I laughed every time I reflected on 3D viewing these photographs in dozens of perspectives, but now my laughter has faded. Nothing has ever sickened me so much, nothing has given me so much vertigo, as having stumbled upon those perverse caricatures and what they wretchedly captured, I tell myself – a perversely distorted world of unrelivable experiences.

Upon my returning from work, from my toil and meticulous, sustained attentiveness to causes and effects, these images exert a dangerous fascination. Nothing is more painful than feeling the lure of pleasure and the threat of pain activate those impulses and appetites that prevent us from realizing that our resistance to obstacles isn't external to us. In that case (0) would play a part at once repellent and depressing. (0) would stimulate these sick desires and weaken me at the same time. Would give me over to nervous emotions without strength to resist them.

I should have forbidden myself from looking at these spectroscopic images from so many different points of view. I should have ignored them, I thought, hastily fumbling through 3D scenes, scene after scene, whose every pixel would shine with the intensity and colour of a holographic memory.

My favourite playlist automatically generated a high-quality depth map. Holograms flicked and shuddered. The rotating library of images evoked faded memories of our escapades against the saturated backdrop of the Mediterranean – abstract imitations of some sunset stippled by stripes of recorded clouds. The hologram sky glittered. My eyes were irrefutably drawn toward the holographic aura of (0), following the familiar outlines of their androgynous body until they came to life again before me. I could visualize it vividly: Their incandescent face rises from a tumble of long black hair, bordered by a blue sky and sea, while protruding genitals cheekily reflect the surrounding landscape of the European tropics. Everything about (0) grew softer and softer in the slippery light of the beach, like clay that has yet to be touched by the sculptor.

It seemed to be the first passion I'd ever known and was probably going to be my last. I hated, despised, and even cursed (0), but the madness of these illusions excited me. I was disgusted with them and disgusted with myself. I swore I'd never see (0) again, but I never thought that I'd be resolved in this.

Love should have followed for (0) and me, but I'm an atheist when it comes to love. Instead of loving, I reason. The forces with which I feared and loved were the forces of a chaos of agonizing atoms of collision and disintegration. We speak of our emotions far beyond the experience we have of them, thinking that without emotion we can live together in any number of ways. Love is always a substitute for the universe, never failing to put us immediately in the universe and the eternity of its freedom, but if it is in fact eternal, it seems to me to be akin to indifference.

Life is so strangely simple. I merely introduced an emotion experimentally, I thought, and was fascinated to see it producing a reaction in another. But in my heart I felt the idiocy of it all. It was all very stupid. The heart is an organ. Each time I gave in to this tempting pain I only added to a disquiet. My dark irritability became something like a bothersome accessory.

We place evil in pleasure. It adorns us, disgusts and horrifies us, excites and seduces us with the greatest powerlessness. What we condemn in love is our own powerlessness. Our sense organs become sensuous organs. And when the temptations of desire offer us an erotic stimulant, we're aroused to embrace the necrophilic, to sink into the fetid, sticky contents of our bodies – sweat, blood, semen, vaginal secretions, excremental discharge. Corpses. The signs of death are the youth of this world of decomposition, whose inner fluids teem with nameless feral life and libidinous microorganisms.

Beyond love, we live in the heartbreaking expression of our past, in the sure decay of hope. For years I've been haunted by these pictures. I felt distracted by my desire for (0), by the passivity of its pangs. A sombre misery twisted and mutilated my feelings until they ceased to be feelings and instead became a kind of drowning in which there was nothing drowned, nor any depth of water that would drown. These feelings were so strange that I gave up on the idea of describing them. They increasingly slipped toward obscurity, and their very slipping was why what disturbed me one day left me indifferent the next.

There are many possibilities of slippage both into and out of love, but I truly believe it could have been anyone and I would have felt the same way. (0) just happened to be this anyone for me. Anyone could have told me what (0) told me, anyone might have offered me that smile. But not just anyone would have smiled at just anyone like that, I thought. When (0) touched me, it was always comforting. Their touch fully contented me. It was a touch that wanted my touch and nothing else. An unlimited fusion. A desire to consume ourselves. A reversal of the pleasant, correct side. Lubricious sensations revealing feelings, parts of the body, and ways of being that we're otherwise ashamed of – showing ourselves that what we show is really impossible to show. We see ourselves with their eyes, feel ourselves with their hands, hear ourselves with their ears. We become visible, become tangible, become audible. Become real.

As I reflected, I watched the visual playlist shudder and dance. Leaving from Rome, we cruised the Mediterranean in a white yacht. We were a world away. The opposition between the beauty of Apollo and the orgy of Dionysus evoked both the figure of the vulgar Venus and the inner sensation of the night's festival tableau.

The yacht docked at the island of Delos for the Delia festival. There was going to be a big party. Ritual licence. Animal avidity. In weather that evaded time we were shown, together with a small number of blasé individuals, the sanctuary of Apollo Delios with its sacred columns, neutral and pure, under the notches of strange hieroglyphs. A buried and barren landscape of stone monsters and the repressed sighs of the regal and attentive marble lions. Gods immobilized in the between-time of art, left for all eternity at the threshold of a future never produced; statues and idols looking at one another with empty eyes that don't see. No one was born or died on the island. Only old, lost divinities. Immortal to the end.

Greece vanished, replaced by Beijing night and the lights of the condos, the high-gloss facades, the terraces and ranked balconies of concrete. The hologram shut off. The projection vanished.

When the primary relationship of our life comes to an end and we awkwardly fit ourselves back into the world, we drop the invisible thread we were following, the path we were exploring, and turn elsewhere. Then we're forced to either hate the world or fail to love it, which comes to the same thing. Without that person we may die, and sometimes we prefer to die rather than be without them.

The whole course of my relationship with (0) could be conceived of in terms of their active membership and my nonmembership in the world transhumanist movement. (0) wanted to become posthuman. And, seeking to contribute to the emergence of a new posthuman form of existence, they disconnected from the human community through radical enhancements – enhancements that eventually created barriers between us, between the *enhanced* and the *mainstream human population.*

You have life-form options, (0) had said. It was my morphological freedom to discover new forms of embodiment, but I couldn't understand the new joys of those technofetishists. If humans can become disconnected from humanity, they cannot be necessarily human, and significant consequences flow from remaining connected, or becoming disconnected. (0) seemed indifferent to much that made existence meaningful to the human they would have been if they hadn't adopted intelligence amplification – things such as Italian food, sex, REM, or landscape painting – and their wayward and cryptic emails implied that they were exploring caverns measureless to humanity.

I only would have needed to become not human. I only would have needed to no longer be human, to seek personal growth beyond my current biological limitations. This would have allowed me unprecedented control over my own nature and morphology – through nanotechnology, biotechnology, information technology, and cognitive science. (0) had become nonhuman. But my oppressive feelings about becoming not human weren't just disconcerting, they were terrifying. Disconnections are an intense becoming, I thought, a becoming that need not be the becoming of something but a becoming without a subject, a becoming that lacked me. An absence in the body.

My bare brain wasn't enough for (0). If I'd become smarter, I would have become better – better at realizing what limited me to being no more intelligent or creative than Newton or Einstein, I thought, because like theirs, the efficiency of my brain was constrained by the speed, interconnectedness, noisiness, and density of the neurons packed into my sapient skull. My mind is just the functional organization of my brain, I thought, a human mind functionally equivalent to any human brain. But I could outsource the tedious tasks of my biological-based cognition to nonbiological platforms by patching computing hardware into the ascension codes of neurocomputational wetware.

Why crawl when you can fly? The idea of perishing pushes the chrysalis to become a butterfly, I thought. Death for the caterpillar consists of receiving the wings of the moth, and there is a consciousness in the mayfly that gives the impression that life will go on forever. (0) gave much more than the life of (0). (0) gave the death of (0). (0) separated themselves from terribly strong feelings of being human, from the terribly agonizing feeling of being a human threatened with death, and changed these feelings into the yet more agonizing feeling of being no longer human. (0) changed so profoundly that it might not have been called a death. Their last moments must have been without any memory. And so all this, their posthuman potentiality and my posthuman predicament, was insignificant.

Outside the window of my Beijing apartment was gloomy nothing. Night thickened into a night beyond night and so did its secrets, summoning the insomniac in me to an abyss that didn't lead back to the day. My head was buzzing. From the sweat moistening my forehead, I knew the alcohol wasn't working anymore. I felt feverish. I probably contracted the virulent disease, I thought. Sickness and infection had entered my body silently, through the open pores on its surfaces. I needed to stop what I was doing and take a pill.

It was useless to struggle against it. I needed only to think of (0), and I did think of (0), and in my grotesque physical attraction for (0), I stuck out my tongue and swallowed a cocktail of liquid pills in the very same way that one swallows the sacred species. I turned off my emotions with stronger and stronger assurances that these emotions didn't hurt in the least, and my feelings of pleasure were over almost as soon as they had begun. It's already gone, I said to myself, as if taking a masochistic oath. This unrelieved disquiet of memories and erotic obsessions is gone.

Everything shut off.

I closed my eyes and the feeling passed. No longer obliged to feel anything, I became myself again. I knew nothing at that moment. I knew nothing about what concerned me, what was important to me. Yet I was conscious of the moment. I was conscious of nothing but the moment. I was in the moment. And, in the grip of the strong emotions that shut me off, I interrupted the flow of my thoughts. In constantly renewed bursts of laughter or tears I stopped thinking. I wept with disgust, I sobbed, I laughed, I gasped.

I sat on the floor, in my suit. For a while I paid attention to the disembodied phases of my unfeeling body as it floated past me. The effect of the substance grew stronger and stronger until I could no longer see anything around me. My body became almost totally insensitive, and I was immersed in a dull, heavy indifference. If I were to be asked about myself in that strange mood, I wouldn't have known if I should be regarded as this living body or the body hovering before me. I was no longer tied to an invisible theme that states itself in the first person but vacillated strangely between *I* and *we*. The word *I* became such an overwhelming semantic event that the possibility of suffering didn't make any sense because there was nothing that was named 'I' to suffer.

The wind continued and so did my illness. The effects of the original dose seemed to have worn off. I felt sick, sicker than I'd ever felt in my life. I felt a pressure in my sinuses. A stifling dryness in my throat. My breath, warmed and moistened by the mucous membranes, streamed between my lips. I'm exposed to the outside by breathing, I thought. By the mucous membrane of my lungs. Now and then my chest gave an uneasy heave, and I would have to cough my bronchial cough.

The air I breathed seemed like layers of hot felt stuffed inside my lungs and head. Suddenly I was overcome by an unspeakable terror of suffocating. A moment later, I could hardly breathe. Sweat trickled down my face, burning like waves of fire. Wet streaks of hair had glued themselves to my forehead. My body was cold, my joints restlessly shaking. I'm doomed to die in quarantine, I thought, and repeatedly mumbled to myself, *Gate gate pāragate pārasamgate bodhi svāhā*, trying to pronounce the phonemes of the foreign language without knowing exactly what the words meant.

In my safe was a gun. I pulled out the gun and would have liked to shoot it, but then I thought shooting it didn't make sense. Then, at that moment, I had a strange experience. I heard the white sound of invasion. I felt a will insinuate itself into my own and I drew back to find I was no longer alone in the depth of my being. A strange will. The sudden intrusion of a precise and discrete desire. It was less complete, less precise than my own interior voice, and yet it was certain, confirming itself without words. Nothing could describe it. It was felt but couldn't be expressed. And my inability to understand it seemed to be an essential part of being human. All was blotted out, its breath disappeared, and I heard nothing. I remained alone with myself, free to obey or not.

I cautiously gripped the cold instrument of death. If I was glad that, or noticed that, or remembered that, or knew that the gun was loaded, then I must have believed that the gun was loaded. Even to wonder whether the gun was loaded, or to speculate on the possibility that the gun was loaded, required the belief that the gun was a weapon, that it was more or less an enduring physical object. There were good reasons for not insisting on wondering whether the gun was loaded. For it certainly wouldn't give the impression that I died by chance.

And it was while I contemplated whether the gun was loaded that an idea began to form. An idea that hadn't quite disengaged itself from the chaos into which the overwhelming death of my family had plunged my mind, and now that idea appeared clearly to me: *I wish for the destruction of the world in my defeat and my death. I wish that the nothingness of death were a void as total as that which would have reigned had the world never been created.*

My mind often formulated these empty concepts, unprincipled and chaotic, and reasoned with content it knew to be fictitious. It elaborated on illusions. A world of preeminently inadequate ideas, unrecognizable objects, and inconsistent phantasms. If I commit suicide, I don't really know what I give myself, I thought. I know only what I reject. The moment I die the memory of this mind, this untranscendable object called me, will be gone. It'll be no trouble at all, tearing this world up by the roots and returning it to the void. All I have to do is die. Death exists. Death is a weapon against this world. It brings the world to destruction. And although I'll be forgotten, in death I'll still have this one effective hostility against the world.

The gun rose. Menace and destruction suit me. I'm the only person I could ever wish to kill. To invert the contact of my soul with my body.

I was already exposed to the gun's bullet by thinking about it. In a sense, I was already obliterated because the hypothetical bullet had already touched the chambers of my heart. No, good violence can only aim at the face . . .

I lowered the gun. It is only after considering the consequences of our suicide that we're troubled, I thought. Enough to not destroy the possibility of ourselves. Only in death can we get out of our own way and see who we really are. But more often than not we're afraid. In our weakness we want to know without dying.

The gun rose again. The present world is one my perceptions have created. A world created by my consciousness. A world to destroy all worlds. In my world, contaminated by me the moment I laid eyes on it, what I really want to see will never happen. I can't get rid of this obstruction, I thought. I can't change the situation without removing myself from the world I share with other people.

I lowered the gun again. We think that no fate can be worse than our own. A fate that is, admittedly, always either going or has already gone, and then another fate that immediately takes form and place out of what has gone, or what has come, or is coming.

I coughed wetly, the muzzle of the gun jerking as I convulsed. I peered at the litter of drugs and alcohol on the table. The combination of alcohol and pills had gotten me tipsy. I wasn't very sure of myself anymore and so, on the point of vomiting, I got up and went to my bedroom to lie down. Disappointed, I lay the gun on my bed. Then I lay down on the black temper foam bed to find blankness again, beside the gun. No, I collapsed in the bed, a mere inert mass. I let my posture dissolve and my legs and arms settle as the force of gravity determined, and eventually I no longer sensed anything, but for a long time, I kept coughing in a ghastly, slimy way, devoid of love, and turning from side to side. Aware and afraid. For this was the void. There was nobody who could help me. Nobody in the world. They were all on something, possible enemies, or dead. My health, meanwhile, grew worse.

I'm already feverish, I thought, already reeling toward my disintegration. In the midst of this feverish, interwoven process of decay, I clasped my chapped hands and rubbed them, a habit that resembled prayer. Because I constantly scrubbed them, they were ominously dry, if not threateningly white. All the same, I'd likely succumbed to an infection no one could escape. I tried to determine the circumstances in which I'd been infected. Only now, using my smartphone as a mirror, did I notice the frightening irritation around my mouth and eyes, followed by the spots on the skin of my entire body. It was impossible to stop and hard to hide, so I looked for other ways to disguise my symptoms from myself.

The wind outside had become wilder. I remained in the same place, deep in thought. And, because I didn't sleep, the night didn't interrupt the flow of time. I suffered from being unable to interrupt the night. The night is real, I thought. And beyond this outer night is an inner night that the day doesn't interrupt or put an end to.

Wakeful but unable to awaken. I longed for sleep.

Swallowing a drink or another pill might put an end to my spell of insomnia, I thought. But the night watches. This insomnia is the psyche that the night invades, and as it invades it extinguishes my personality, my identity, replacing it with a visible night, an auditory night, an olfactory night, a tactile night. In the heart of the night, I maintain an anonymous vigilance that watches where there is nothing to watch for. My insomnia is the impossibility of slipping away and distracting myself from my disquiet. My insomnia is not an insomnia of consciousness but of obsession.

Sleep wouldn't come. When it did come later, I woke repeatedly. But with it came dreams. It brought dreams that cast a shaft of light on the spiral of night. I dreamed that it was early spring and raining, a sad, lonely rain dropping from the trees like black liquid in a pine grove beneath the storm. And as I dreamed, it seemed to me that I was stopped at the edge of the woods from my childhood. And so I headed into the woods, along a path of wet pine needles.

I floated in the centre of a forest dominated by emerald green arches of foliage. In the forest, water seeped, trickled, dribbled everywhere. The path I took was the only one available and descended into the valley. It was a firm earthen path, reddish in colour and a little damp, with boulders here and there along the edge. The sky shone like a deep blue velvet above the spear-shaped tops of the pines, and I wandered the slopes and gazed at the long, rain-cooled grass.

I walked down the path to get somewhere, but I realized I could just enjoy walking nowhere. I smelled water everywhere, and the spongy earth beneath me. The crust of the mossy forest floor summoned realms of events and epiphanies. A mist floated among the fir trees. Sometimes, when I stopped, I could hear, among the wet pine trees, in the stillness of the high forest, plethoric drops joining to make a waterfall.

Water beat faintly in the distance like a call of inexpressible sorrow, an echo of transcendence. It was an impression I had as I moved forward along this needle-strewn path, the sound of my goal louder in my ear as I neared it. A bumping and hissing, a gradually increasing rumble. Pursuing it led me relentlessly downhill toward the cliff path. There was a delicate excitement offered by the slopes, in the changing distribution of the flora, in the approach of the waterfall, in the trails and the waters plunging forever downward into a chasm in which the churning water boiled and roared over black boulders. I could smell the damp rising from the waterfall and the odour of mould, an almost abstract smell.

I turned to look beyond the tree trunks to the mountains and caught sight of the white monolith of the waterfall. The earth showed its bones in a kind of geological metaphor. A turn in the path revealed a rocky forest ravine and the waterfall leaping down it. Masses of water plunged down in a single vertical cascade, in a maddening cacophony of every conceivable noise. As the water fell and broke, by emanation and descent, the delicate changes of that sombre stream, which had hidden and concealed its aggression and agitation, came down stern and hard upon the plunge pool with glacial ferocity.

And so it fell, like a severed head. The water, having lost its serenity, became an uneasy white foam that hurried on in some confusion as it trailed off toward the sea. Vast, fleeting sheets of spray hurled like an apology over the gaping mouth of this dark and sullen pool. For an instant the sacred white noise of the falls was a manifest vision of a bright-white nothing. The beautiful white colour of the water had more and more of the colour of death. It became an ugly alienation from a sacred world.

I descended the ravine on whose top I stood, so that I could view the water from down below. It was difficult. A series of steep, narrow steps hewn into the rock led down to the lower story of the woods. I then walked out onto the bridge of stones that hovered just above the curl of the falls. I crossed the stones across the rapids and made the more arduous descent on the other side. The brush made me crouch and I had to forget about the mud and the thorns to make my way through it. There were side walls to climb, and I felt my way across the unstable rocks of the harsh ridges of the mountain paths, felt the warmth and the dampness of the earth with the soles of my leather boots. I groped at the rocks as the masses of my hands pressed up against them and skidded across their gritty relief.

Halfway down the cliff, at a place where a narrow ledge made it possible, I forced myself to pause and turn to face an emptiness of space that induced vertigo. A cold sweat started on my forehead, and my hands grew dangerously slippery. I shut my eyes to avoid seeing the terrestrial depths. My body was the elevation itself. But then I opened them again, resolved to conquer my weakness, and it occurred to me as I did so to look for that foothold of clay or granite, slate or silica, whose distance at once terrified and attracted me.

I'd reached the base of the cliff only from the cliff, by a rope ladder. Holes were bored into the wall of rock, and in the rock were grainy outlines with beautiful, sparkling round crystal ornaments. A sense of comfort instantly restored some part of my faculties. Below, the waterfall unfolded and noisily burst from the gorge. On all sides rose reddish cliffs. A dense mist that had surged in waves from the gorge completely covered everything, and not a single sound reached me besides the muffled resonance contained within it. I could hear the rustling of nothingness, back into which the waters flowed and were lost. And since the real world, the world populated by human beings, very quickly closed its door behind me and was lost from sight, and since no sound could reach me from down here now, I was more deeply lost than I could ever have wished.

I don't know how to describe that moment in words. It was extreme and it was horrifying.

I'd almost reached the bottom of the natural stairway, and there, right in view of the falls, was something like a flowing stream. Some torrents flowed chrome, others black, others glowed with all the colours of the rainbow. My eyes were unable to keep up with the confusion of shape and colour, the madly swirling shades and metapatterns that raged before me. The light it cast was extremely bright, but there was nothing blinding or frightening about it. Simply watching the constant emergence of new multicoloured sparks and glimmers of light was enough to convey a very real impression of infinitely powerful grace, happiness, and love. The necessary unity of mind and nature in a singular pleroma, a pattern that connected everything. Everything I could possibly think of or dream of was part of that rainbow-hued stream. And the rainbow-hued stream was in turn everything that I could possibly think or experience, everything that I could possibly be or not be, and I knew that it was not something separate from me.

It was I, and I was it. I had always been it, and nothing else.

Feeling a wave of exhilaration as the rushing current shivered and blurred and gelled, I saw (0). There (0) stood, clearly visible beside the cliff that slid down into cold mist and the sound of rapids. It was (0), really, though they no longer had the face or the body of a human being but were a mixture of insect, tree, and earth. Then something nongeometric, vaguely like a human face, filled the absence. Covered with the hypothetically intricate traceries of bewitching rainbows, delicate arches of shifting polychrome stretched across an expanse of asymmetrical features. Hideous in its imperfection, I cast a look of horror on this alien being who, in obedience to an order beyond my comprehension, was both considerate of my temperament and my individual character by placing itself on the level of my intellect in the only material form that I could have conceived of. This being had assumed the simple aspect of the person I loved most.

Its blank face swirled like smoke, towering above me, and took an outline that began to seethe with faint internal shadows. And suddenly (0) spoke. Blue and scarlet lips parted wetly as the twisted, elongated jaw moved. But it was impossible to hear its voice over the waterfall, amid the thunder, and its mouth formed words that remained soundless. (0) walked over to me, came very close to me, tried to say something else, but no words would come from its lips. A superhuman expression illuminated the gangrenous flesh and convulsed features, shot through with greenish-purple flashes of pain. Then (0) became transparent, and through its face filtered the obscure gleam of light coming from beyond its face, from what was not yet, from a future not future enough. Something, perhaps a hand, a thing like a clump of roots, fumbled toward me, blurred, and vanished.

"Wait!" I said, frightened. "You can't leave me like this. You must explain..." But it was too late. (0) went back into the rainbow-hued radiance. It parted for a moment like water and then closed over (0), and I was left alone.

For a few minutes I stared, stunned, at the spot where (0) had been. No sooner had (0) departed than the radiance surrounding me faded. The rainbow turned black. What had emanated celestial joy and spiritual calm became acute anguish and turmoil. All I felt now was fear, a generalized dread. Scrambling over the slippery rocks, I moved closer and stood there wet with spray, wrapped in the aura of the waterfall's own misty vapour. My ears were baffled by the deafening, insane, extravagant roar. I stared at the surging waters, reversing irreversible time in vortices, a catastrophe of hurling foam in which everything ended in confusion. From the deepest shadows there rose a prolonged cry, which was the end of the dream.

I'd never heard anything like that sound. A sort of bubbling wail of raw and total fear.

And then I woke up, bathed in sweat, my body thrown into confusion. The fever had been fierce, in all its stages. I simply lay there blinking, my dream already dissolving. And by the time I got up I was no longer exactly sure what my thoughts had been.

Once I woke fully from the confusing dream of (0), I was unable to recall who (0) was or what (0) ever meant to me. When I remembered, I saw what I'd been looking at the night before – an unloaded gun – and picked up the thread that had been dropped but was unbroken. This idea of suicide, which had taken possession of me for the night, also dissolved, and there remained only a startled excitement that nothing could account for.

We wake up and the world is different, though nothing has changed.

Sunday came. I went into the bathroom and brushed my teeth. As I was stepping out, the monitor on the main room's audiovisual complex lit up. I put on my virtual headset.   Onscreen the ceremony video connection had been made, and when the screen displaying the feed for the funeral came online, I went live and found myself looking at the dead faces of my family. By now my family no longer had human faces at all, but nonhuman faces. I looked into these faces that should probably be covered, and my detestation of the human face grew even fiercer than before. I could hardly recognize my family in those bodies that were before me, and I doubted whether they'd ever really possessed them.

I gave no response when asked to speak about the depressing-looking corpses bearing makeup. Like every other body at a funeral, each was cleaned and made pretty. They were now mortuary objects, and somehow belonged to the cemetery. They would soon disappear under vegetation, become discoloured, amorphous, and incomprehensible.

Dandelions grew between the rows of graves, and mushrooms appeared around the columns of tombs. An infinity of holes, all in the shape of people. Hollowed-out outlines of the beings it lacked. One can find no place more significant than a cemetery, I thought, where a person's life is so swiftly disposed of and hidden from the public gaze. We try to place the beyond at a safe and distant remove, but our effort is futile, and we are always shocked afresh by the depth of those open graves, which frighten us every time.

The coffins were lowered one by one into their underground heaven. During the burial, I looked only at the strangely dark pits with tombstone photographs in porcelain frames that portrayed the family plot. I felt no emotion as they were put into the ground, nor integrated it when the holes were filled with soil. Because just as they were buried in the ground, so too were they buried in the inaccessible parts of my fossil memories.

In fact, I no longer remembered them. A weakness of memory, an incapacity to cross large intervals of time, to resuscitate pasts too deep. The tombstones were high, topped with a cross, and there was a place where the head of Christ, this god of the morgue, was in a crown of thorns, without aureole, without nimbus. Around the grave, an iron fence. They lay separately, some distance between them, and yet they rotted altogether in this grave. Alongside profane and sacred time, they rotted body and soul. A fitting punishment, I thought, for them to lie in a cemetery, a tactile void. On the plaque an inscription was carved: *Above the souls of the dead stands Christ.* It was Sunday, the sun was shining, but nothing suggested that by some miracle my family would return to life on Monday.

There's a beginning and an end to every circle. But we're all going around and around in the most depressing circles. Because the beginning and end of a circle are one. We don't know what started it all. But something in us does, and we just go on with our lives, endlessly. Eternally. Because there's no such thing as death. We can only profit from the momentum of our fall for as long as it lasts. For the first time, it seemed as though I were responsible for their mortality, and guilty of surviving.

The people inside the expensive wood and metal coffins were merely my imagination, I told myself. A coffin is a piece of furniture. No more than the senseless luxury and excess of death. Everything they'd felt and experienced in this life, in this world, was now in these coffins of experience.

The wind stirred the grass and the cypresses, giving me the sensation of an internal, visceral emptiness, as the corpses whispered their truth. All around, the vegetation grew. In early spring, when things begin to bloom, it's as if the dead really do persist. But the newness of springtimes that flower in the instant are already heavy with all the springtimes lived through. Nourishing ghosts of weeds. Their bodies did this, I thought. Deprived of voice, sight, motion, they sought to communicate through their decomposition, through their corpses.

The weight of their deaths had finally reached me. The cemetery is within me, I thought. Our dead are inside us. They emerge through our eyes, our ears, our mouth... Suddenly I had trouble breathing, as if I were choking on reality. This inevitable movement of systole and diastole, the heart beating fully against the walls of my skin, had stopped, and I felt the density of my own existence. I rushed to the bathroom and vomited.

Kneeling next to the white enamel toilet, I placed my face in the hollows of my hands – so hollow that I descended into myself, as if underground, closed my eyes, and began to cry. I began to really sob the uncontrollable tide of sobs that I'd stifled, kneeling on the cold tiled floor of the bathroom, in the sterile smell of cleanliness and hygiene. I am alone, I thought. It was here and only here, in the bathroom, like an empty confessional, that I could be alone for a while and find both peace and tranquility.

I need solitude, to just be by myself, as in my childhood, I thought. To be alone, as in my entire life. I am more alone without solitude.

Death was unable to maintain its icy little horror, here, next to the toilet of my Beijing apartment. Then I pressed the flush button, as if to signal that I'd finished my business, and I silently set off to continue participating in the livestream, which was still streaming.

I eventually found an excuse to leave the gathering. On leaving, I thought: Their death is no longer anything to me. Whatever connected me to it was uniformly detestable. My eyes had touched the dead things lightly, just enough to recognize on them the function the program of our everyday concerns put on them. But when I looked beneath this human function, reducing them from a past fact to an actual image, I saw prefigurations of its other side, the side I left behind discoloured, bulged, shrivelled, and disintegrated. At this I took off the virtual headset. "Idiots," I whispered, turning my face to watch the blank wall that screened Beijing and feeling tears of helpless hatred for the world welling in my burning eyes.

Things will gradually return to their proper place, I thought, and this will allow me to feel that I have survived, to provide me with a break from a reality I don't understand and don't particularly care for. A reality, my reality, that has assumed, more and more, the aspect of the afterlife.

In fact, I'd firmly resolved to make an appointment to meet with the hologram of a transhumanist in the Pudong district of Shanghai, intending to offer the whole of myself, just as I stood, with everything belonging to me. An unconditional offering to the transhumanist community in Shanghai.

I met the transhumanist two days after the funeral, and they accepted me on behalf of the transhumanist community. From Beijing, where I no longer live, where I wrote this work entitled *Disconnection*, and where I never intended to stay, writes Théodore Ostrom, I thanked them for accepting me.